HOT HIPPO

Author's note for readers : the name Ngai
should be pronounced N-guy.

Also by Mwenye Hadithi and Adrienne Kennaway:

Baby Baboon
Crafty Chameleon
Greedy Zebra
Lazy Lion
Tricky Tortoise

First Paperback Edition

Library of Congress Cataloging-in-Publication Data
Mwenye Hadithi.
   Hot Hippo.

   Summary: Relates why the hippopotamus lives in water.
   (1. Hippopotamus-Fiction) I. Moore, Adrienne, ill.
   II. Title.
PZ7.M975Ho 1986   (E)   86-65
ISBN 0-316-33722-6 (hc)
ISBN 0-316-33718-8 (pb)

10 9 8 7 6 5 4 3 2

Printed in Belgium

HOT HIPPO

by **Mwenye Hadithi**

Illustrated by **Adrienne Kennaway**

Little, Brown and Company
Boston   New York   Toronto   London

Hippo was hot.

He sat on the river bank and
gazed at the little fishes
swimming in the water.

If only I could live in the water, he thought, how wonderful life would be.

So he walked and he ran and he strolled
and he hopped and he lumbered along until he
came to the mountain where Ngai lived.

Ngai was the god of
Everything and Everywhere.

Ngai told the animals to live on the land and the fishes to live in the sea.

Ngai told the birds to fly in the air
and the ants to live under the ground.

Ngai had told Hippo he was to live on the land and eat grass.

"Please, O great Ngai, god of Everything and Everywhere, I would so much like to live in the rivers and streams," begged Hippo hopefully. "I would still eat grass."

"Aha!" thundered the voice of Ngai.
"So you say. But one day you might,
just might, eat a fish to see if it
tasted good. And then you would
EAT ALL MY LITTLE FISHES!"

"Oh no, I promise I wouldn't,"
said Hippo.
"Aha!" thundered the voice of Ngai.
"So you say! But how can I be sure of that?
I LOVE MY LITTLE FISHES!"

"I would show you," promised Hippo.
"I will let you look in my mouth whenever you like,
to see that I am not eating your little fishes.

"And I will stir up the water with my tail so you can see I have not hidden the bones."

"Aha!" thundered the voice of Ngai. "Then you may live in the water but…" Hippo waited…

"… But you must come out of the water at night and eat grass, so that even in the dark I can tell you are not eating my little fishes. Agreed?"
"Agreed!" sang Hippo happily.

And he ran all the way home
until he got to the river,
where he jumped in
with a mighty SPLASH!

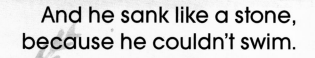

And he sank like a stone,
because he couldn't swim.

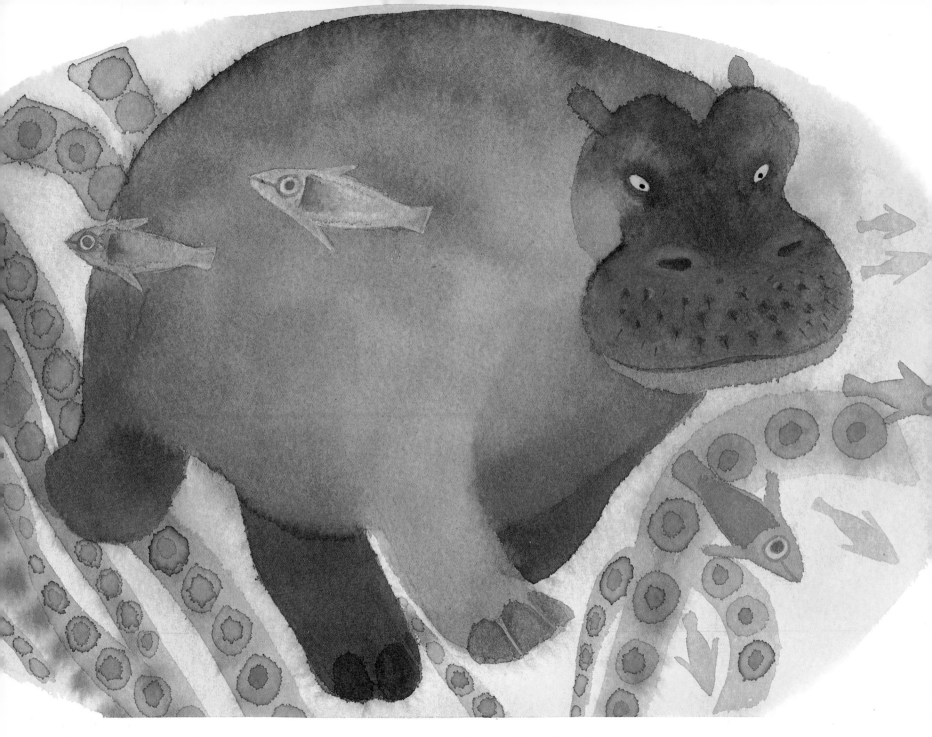

But he could hold his breath and run along the bottom
which he does to this very day.

And he stirs up the bottom by wagging his little tail,
so that Ngai can see he has not hidden
any fish-bones.

And now and then he floats to the top
and opens his huge mouth ever so wide
and says: "Look, Ngai! No fishes!"